Bo the Bear BUILDS a Race car

REBECCA AND JAMES MCDONALD

Bo the Bear Builds a Race Car

ISBN: 978-0-9982949-5-7

First House of Lore paperback edition, 2018

Visit us at www.HouseOfLore.net

Way back in the woods lived a bear named Bo. Bo loved to be busy. When he wasn't wandering and looking for new things to do, Bo was busy building.

Bo the Bear loved to learn and think about interesting things, like how to safely get honey from a beehive or how to catch a fish without getting wet.

As Bo wandered and pondered, he came upon an old garage with a race track that circled around it.

Bo the Bear had always wanted to drive a car, and what better car to drive than a race car! He rushed into the garage and stumbled to a stop. There were no race cars, only old car parts lying around.

Bo rolled forward four tires and dusted off an old fender. Were there enough parts to build a race car? Bo decided to get to work and find out!

But where would he start? Lucky for Bo there was a stack of books that showed how to build a race car, so he pulled up a car seat and began to read.

Bo read every page of every book and then started over again. Finally, when he looked around the garage, he saw all the parts he would need.

The first thing Bo needed to do was clean the garage. It would be easier to build when things weren't such a mess.

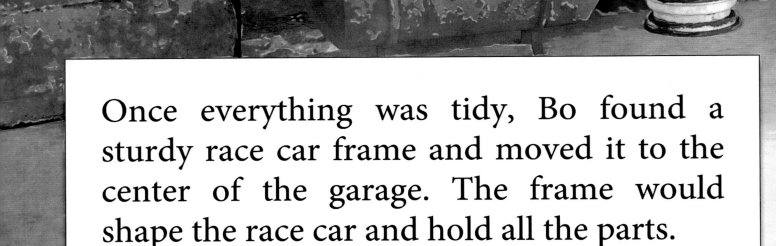

Once everything was tidy, Bo found a sturdy race car frame and moved it to the center of the garage. The frame would shape the race car and hold all the parts.

Next, Bo put on the wheels and suspension. Wheels would help the race car move, and suspension would help the race car drive smoothly over bumps.

Bo built up the frame of the race car, attached the bumpers and fenders, and put on the doors. If there was a crash, they would help protect the driver.

Bo found a powerful engine and set it in place on the frame. The engine would make the race car go.

Bo the Bear stopped and scratched his head. He knew he needed something that would send the engine's power to the wheels, but he couldn't remember what. He flipped through the old books and found them, a transmission and a drivetrain!

A fast engine could overheat, so Bo installed a radiator and hoses to keep it cool. Next went the gas tank to hold the gas and the battery and wires for light.

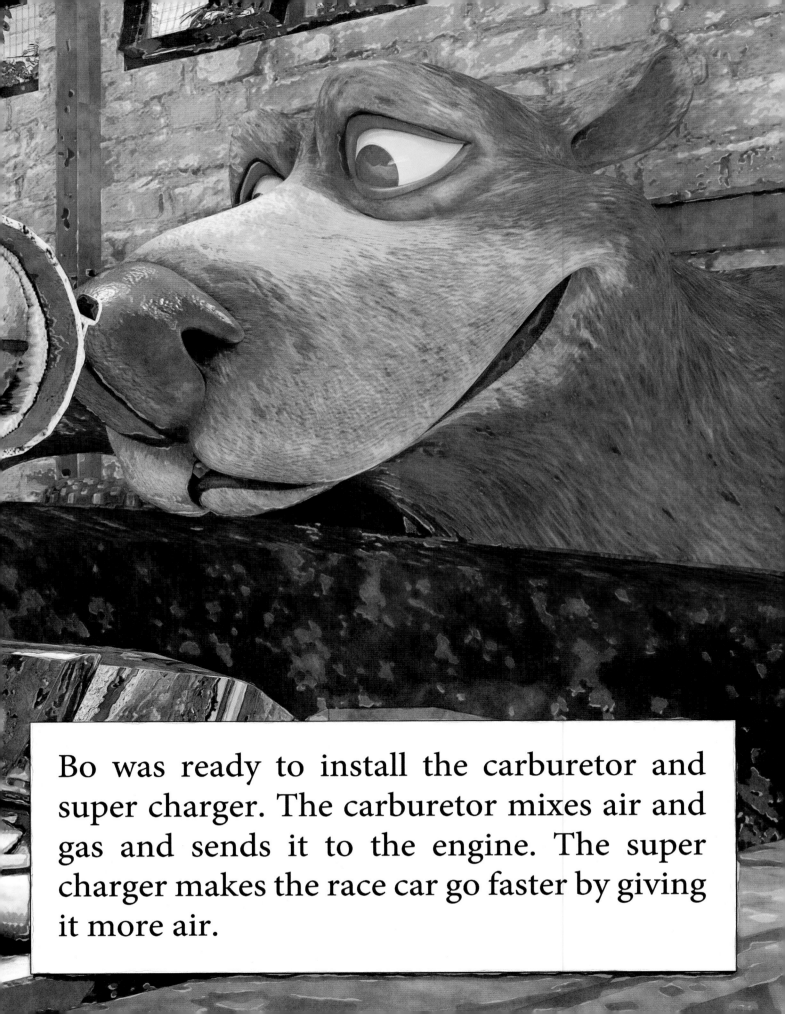

Bo was ready to install the carburetor and super charger. The carburetor mixes air and gas and sends it to the engine. The super charger makes the race car go faster by giving it more air.

Bo pulled a dusty old muffler from a pile of parts. Mufflers quiet the noise of the engine. Bo the Bear laughed at the idea of a quiet race car and tossed the muffler back on the pile. His engine would be the loudest!

Bo installed the seats and then carefully picked up the windshield and set it in place. The windshield would keep rocks and bugs from hitting his face. Then, he put the hood on to protect the engine from rain.

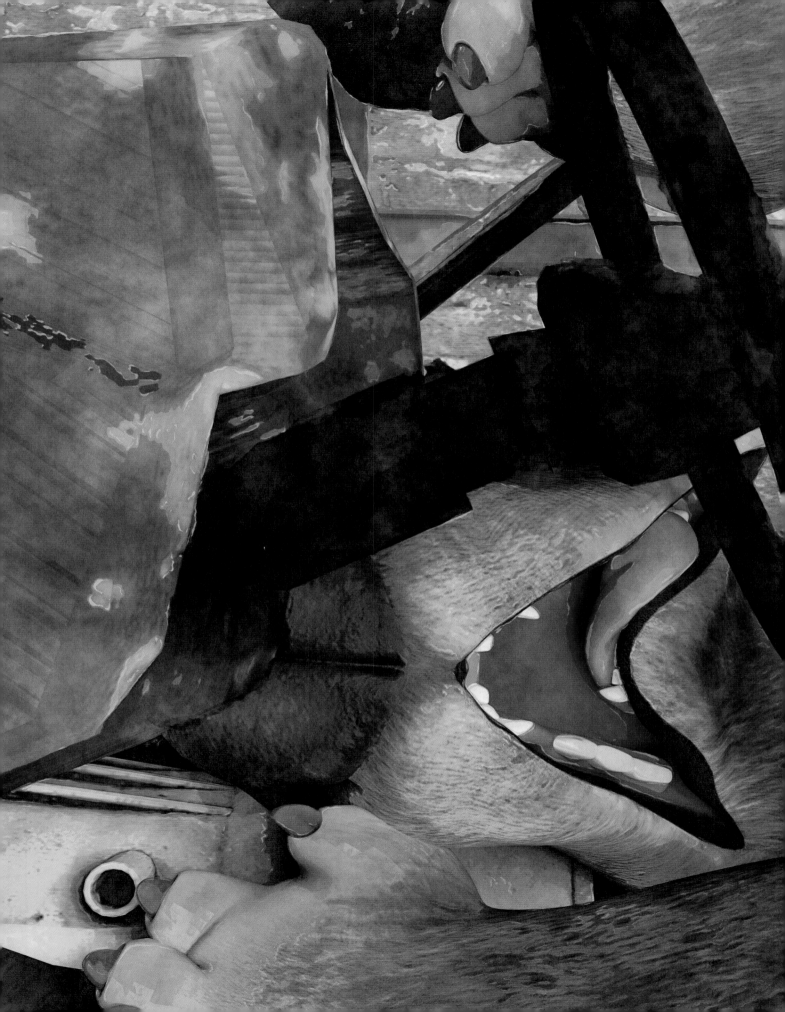

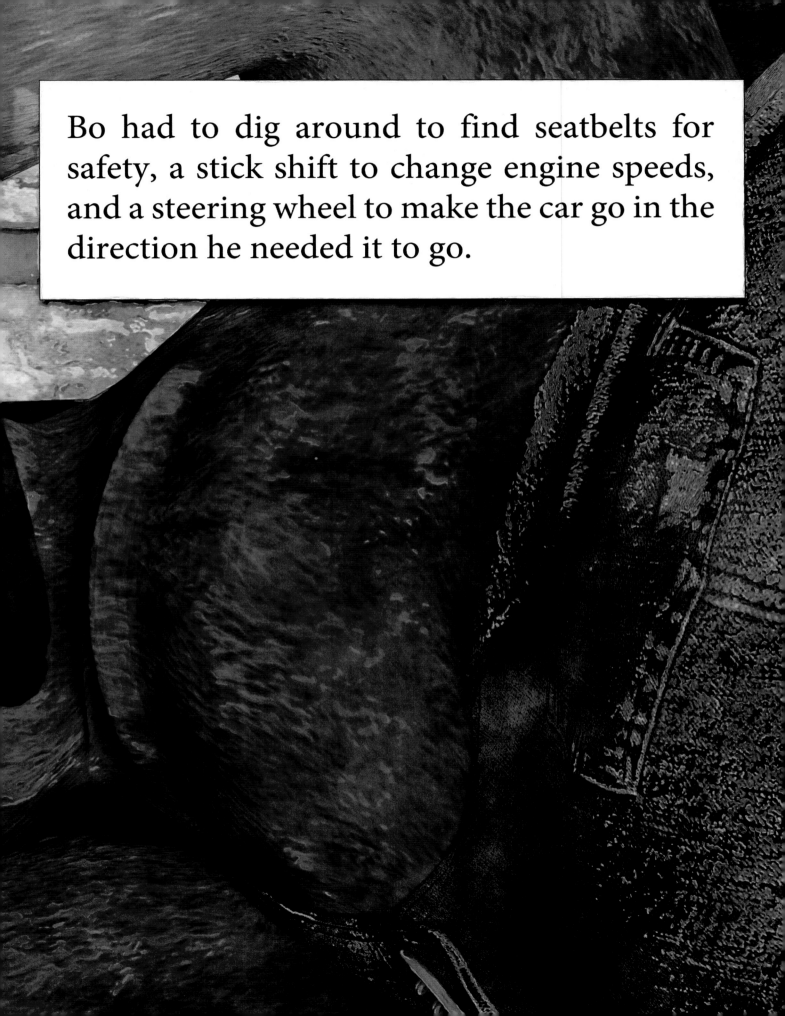

Bo had to dig around to find seatbelts for safety, a stick shift to change engine speeds, and a steering wheel to make the car go in the direction he needed it to go.

Bo stood back and looked at his race car. Wait a second, something was missing. He almost forgot the paint. He found his favorite color in a can under a shelf. Bo the Bear would paint his race car orange!

Bo installed the gas, brake, and clutch pedals. They make the car stop and go. Then Bo filled all the fluids. Finally, the race car was ready to drive! He put in the key and gave it a turn.

It started on the first try.

Bo drove slowly out of the garage and onto the old race track. He checked the area to make sure it was safe. Once he was sure it was all clear, Bo was on his way!

The tires peeled out as Bo the Bear raced around the track. He raced and raced until his car almost ran out of gas.

As Bo came around the last corner, he stepped on it, and all the sudden, the car was on two wheels!

Bo drove all the way into the garage on those two wheels and came to a stop right in the center.

Bo the Bear did it! He built a race car, and now it was time for him to clean up his mess. Bo had so much fun building the race car that he was ready to build something else.

What would it be next time?

The End

I Am
the Sun
REBECCA AND JAMES MCDONALD

I Am
Earth
Rebecca and James McDonald

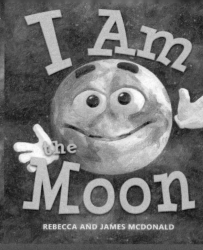

I Am
the Moon
REBECCA AND JAMES MCDONALD

I Am
Mars
REBECCA AND JAMES MCDONALD

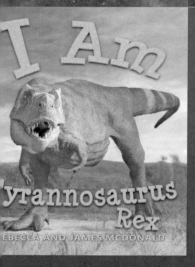

I AM
Tyrannosaurus Rex
REBECCA AND JAMES MCDONALD

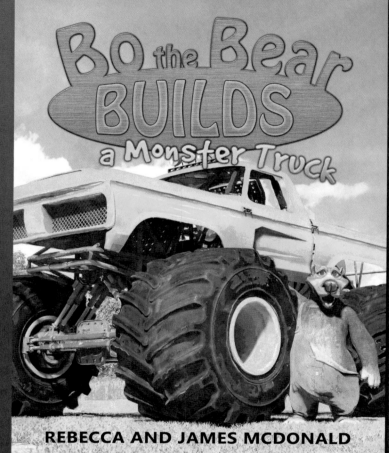

Bo the Bear
BUILDS
a Monster Truck
REBECCA AND JAMES MCDONALD

I AM
Triceratops
REBECCA AND JAMES MCDONALD

I Am
A Bee
REBECCA AND JAMES MCDONALD

I Am
Spring
REBECCA AND JAMES MCDONALD

Rainy Day Poems

Through The Milky Way
On A PB&J

I AM
A Dinosaur

Sometime
I Feel

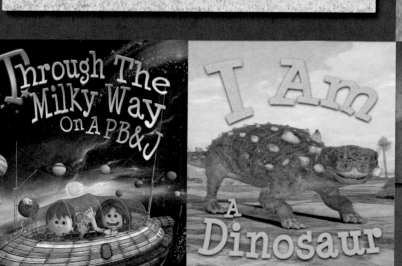